Top Ten Legendary NBA Players

By *Mike Bhangu*

____

Published by BB Productions

British Columbia, Canada

thinkingmanmike@gmail.com

Top Ten Legendary NBA Players

Table of Contents

Introduction

Step into the arena, where the roar of the crowd echoes and the hardwood glistens under the spotlight. Here, giants walk among mortals, defying physical limitations and leaving audiences breathless with their displays of athletic prowess and sheer basketball genius. In this realm, names like Larry Bird, Tim Duncan, Kobe Bryant, and Shaquille O'Neal resonate with awe and admiration. Each player, with their own unique style and set of accomplishments, has etched their name into the annals of basketball history, leaving behind legacies that continue to inspire generations of players and fans alike.

This book embarks on a journey through these legendary figures' careers, exploring their remarkable achievements, fascinating statistics, and captivating stories. We delve into their statistical dominance, highlighting their individual strengths and contributions that made them champions on the court. But statistics only tell part of the story. We uncover rare facts and trivia, shedding light on their personalities, challenges, and triumphs that paint a vivid picture of each player's journey.

Beyond the individual narratives, we explore the broader impact these legends have had on the game. From Larry Bird's "Hick from French Lick" persona and iconic trash-talking to Tim Duncan's quiet leadership and "Big Fundamental" approach, each player has left an indelible mark on the culture and evolution of basketball. Their influence extends far beyond the scoreboards, inspiring countless individuals with their dedication, passion, and unwavering commitment to achieving greatness.

Prepare to be captivated by tales of phenomenal talent, fierce competition, and moments that have become etched in the collective memory of basketball fans worldwide. This book is a celebration of the legends who have shaped the game, leaving behind a legacy that will continue to ignite passion and inspire generations to come.

Reasoning for the Top 10

This list of the top 10 NBA players of all time is based on several key factors.

1. Statistical Dominance: Each player on the list has achieved remarkable statistical feats, including championships won, MVP awards, scoring titles, and other individual accolades. These statistics serve as objective measures of their dominance and impact on the game.

2. Longevity and Consistency: Many players on the list have enjoyed long and successful careers, consistently performing at an elite level for over a decade. This longevity showcases their dedication, work ethic, and ability to adapt to the changing landscape of the NBA.

3. Impact on the Game: Several players on the list have made significant contributions beyond their individual achievements. They have redefined positions, revolutionized playing styles, and inspired generations of players with their unique talents and leadership.

4. Cultural Significance: Some players transcend the sport and become cultural icons, influencing fashion, music, and popular culture. This wider impact elevates their legacy and solidifies their place among the all-time greats.

5. Championship Pedigree: While individual statistics are important, championships are the ultimate measure of success in the NBA. Players like Bill Russell and Michael Jordan, who have multiple championships to their names, demonstrate a winning mentality and clutch performance under pressure.

6. Versatility and Skill Set: Some players possess a unique combination of skills and abilities that make them nearly impossible to defend. Magic Johnson's passing vision, Kobe Bryant's offensive arsenal, and Tim Duncan's defensive prowess are prime examples of this versatility, which makes them even more valuable to their teams.

7. Intangibles: Factors like leadership, competitive spirit, and basketball IQ also play a significant role in determining a player's greatness. Michael Jordan's unwavering determination, Kareem Abdul-Jabbar's calm demeanor under pressure, and LeBron James' ability to elevate his teammates are examples of these intangible qualities that set them apart.

8. Historical Context: While comparing players from different eras can be challenging, it's important to consider the historical context of their accomplishments. Wilt Chamberlain's dominance in a less physical era, Bill Russell's impact in a completely different style of play, and Kareem Abdul-Jabbar's longevity over 20 seasons are all remarkable achievements in their respective eras.

Chapter 1: Top 10 NBA Players

It is important to note that this list is inherently subjective and there will always be differing opinions and players who could be included. However, the individuals listed below have all achieved remarkable feats, left a lasting impact on the game, and are widely recognized as some of the greatest basketball players to ever grace the court.

1. Michael Jordan: Widely considered the greatest basketball player of all time, Jordan dominated the league in the 90s with his incredible scoring ability, athleticism, and competitive spirit. He won six NBA championships with the Chicago Bulls and five MVP awards.

2. Kareem Abdul-Jabbar: The NBA's all-time leading scorer, Abdul-Jabbar was a dominant force for over two decades with his unstoppable skyhook shot. He won six NBA championships, six MVP awards, and was a 19-time All-Star.

3. Bill Russell: The ultimate winner, Russell led the Boston Celtics to a staggering 11 NBA championships in 13 seasons. He was a defensive powerhouse and a key contributor to the Celtics' dynasty.

4. Wilt Chamberlain: An unstoppable force of nature, Chamberlain holds numerous NBA records, including the most points scored in

a single game (100) and the most rebounds in a career. He was dominant despite playing in a much different era of basketball.

5. LeBron James: Considered one of the most complete basketball players ever, James has been a dominant force in the league for over two decades. He has won four NBA championships, four MVP awards, and is still playing at an elite level at age 38.

6. Magic Johnson: A revolutionary point guard, Johnson led the Showtime Lakers to five NBA championships with his incredible passing, vision, and leadership. His impact on the game goes far beyond his statistics.

7. Larry Bird: "The Hick from French Lick" was one of the most skilled and versatile players ever. He won three NBA championships with the Boston Celtics and is considered one of the greatest shooters in NBA history.

8. Tim Duncan: The "Big Fundamental" was the cornerstone of the San Antonio Spurs dynasty, winning five NBA championships and two MVP awards. He was a dominant force on both ends of the court and is considered one of the greatest power forwards ever.

9. Kobe Bryant: "The Black Mamba" was a fierce competitor and one of the most skilled offensive players ever. He won five NBA

championships with the Los Angeles Lakers and is considered one of the greatest shooting guards ever.

10. Shaquille O'Neal: "Shaq" was an unstoppable force in the paint during his prime. He won four NBA championships, three with the Los Angeles Lakers and one with the Miami Heat. His combination of size, strength, and skill made him one of the most dominant centers ever.

This list is subjective and there are many other players who could be considered for this list. However, these ten players are widely considered to be among the greatest of all time.

Chapter 2: Michael Jordan

"The Undisputed King of Basketball"

Michael Jordan's reign as the most iconic basketball player of all time is built on a foundation of undeniable talent, relentless drive, and an insatiable hunger for victory. But beyond the well-known stats and championships lies a treasure trove of lesser-known facts that illuminate the extraordinary depth of his genius and the sheer force of his will.

Statistical Dominance

- 6 NBA championships with the Chicago Bulls (1991-1993, 1996-1998)
- 5 NBA Most Valuable Player Awards (1991, 1992, 1996, 1998, 2001)
- 6 NBA Finals MVP Awards (1991, 1992, 1993, 1996, 1997, 1998)
- 10 NBA scoring titles
- 14 NBA All-Star appearances
- 9 NBA All-Defensive First Team selections
- 2 Olympic Gold Medals (1984, 1992)

Interesting Facts

- Ambidextrous: Jordan could write and shoot with both hands equally well, a rare trait that gave him an edge in certain situations.

- Fear of Failure: Despite his confident public persona, Jordan battled a deep fear of failure throughout his career. This fear fueled his intense work ethic and competitive drive.

- Pre-game Rituals: Jordan had a strict pre-game routine that included listening to specific music, wearing lucky socks, and chewing gum.

- Extreme Competitiveness: Jordan's competitive spirit extended beyond basketball. He was known to be a ruthless competitor in everything he did, from card games to golf.

- Marketing Genius: Jordan's marketability is unmatched in sports history. He partnered with Nike to create the iconic Air Jordan brand, which transformed the sports apparel industry.

- Cultural Icon: Jordan's impact goes far beyond the basketball court. He is a global icon who has transcended sports and become a symbol of success, determination, and style.

- Perfect Record in the Finals: Jordan never lost an NBA Finals series. He won all six Finals he participated in, solidifying his legacy as the ultimate winner.

- Clutch Performance: Jordan's ability to perform on the biggest stage was legendary. He earned the nickname "His Airness" for his seemingly impossible last-minute shots.

- Business Acumen: Jordan is a successful businessman with investments in various ventures, including the Charlotte Hornets NBA team.

- Philanthropy: Jordan is a dedicated philanthropist who supports various charities through his foundation.

The Legacy of a Champion

Michael Jordan's impact on the game of basketball is immeasurable. He has inspired generations of players with his incredible talent, unwavering dedication, and relentless pursuit of excellence. His legacy as the greatest basketball player ever will continue to inspire athletes and fans for years to come.

A Michael Jordan Story

Michael Jordan, despite his intense on-court persona, was also known for his playful and mischievous side. Here's a funny story from his playing days.

During a practice session, Jordan noticed a young rookie watching him intently. The rookie, eager to impress, was trying to mimic Jordan's every move. With a playful glint in his eye, Jordan decided to have some fun. He started making exaggeratedly difficult shots, including fadeaways from impossible angles and no-look passes that went nowhere near their intended target.

The rookie, believing this was the true essence of Jordan's greatness, tried to replicate these impossible feats. As expected, he air-balled several shots and threw passes that landed out of bounds. All the while, Jordan watched with amusement, a sly smile playing on his lips.

Finally, after a particularly disastrous attempt by the rookie, Jordan couldn't hold back his laughter any longer. He burst out laughing and patted the rookie on the back, saying, "Don't worry, kid. I don't even make those shots in practice!"

The young player looked sheepish for a moment, but then he too started to laugh. He realized that Jordan was just messing with him and that even the greatest basketball player in the world doesn't make every shot. This playful interaction not only broke the ice between Jordan and the rookie but also served as a valuable lesson about humility and not taking oneself too seriously.

This story highlights Jordan's ability to connect with his teammates, even the rookies, through humor and lightheartedness. It shows that he wasn't just a serious competitor but also someone who enjoyed the game and knew how to laugh at himself, making him even more relatable and inspiring.

Chapter 3: Kareem Abdul-Jabbar

"The Unstoppable Skyhook"

Kareem Abdul-Jabbar, known as Lew Alcindor in college, stands tall as a legendary figure in basketball history. His towering presence, unparalleled skill, and unyielding determination cemented his place amongst the greatest to ever grace the court. Beyond the well-known accolades, hidden gems and rare facts illuminate the depth of his basketball genius and the profound impact he made on the game.

Statistical Brilliance

- NBA's All-Time Leading Scorer with 38,387 points
- 6 NBA Championships (1971 with Milwaukee Bucks, 1980, 1982, 1985, 1987, 1988 with Los Angeles Lakers)
- 6 NBA Most Valuable Player Awards (1971, 1972, 1974, 1976, 1977, 1980)
- 19 NBA All-Star appearances
- 15 NBA All-Defensive First Team selections
- 6 NBA blocks titles
- 2 Olympic Gold Medals (1964, 1968)

Interesting Facts

- Martial Arts Master: Abdul-Jabbar is a trained martial artist, holding a black belt in Jeet Kune Do, which he credits for improving his footwork and agility.

- Polyglot: Abdul-Jabbar speaks four languages fluently: English, Arabic, Swahili, and Yoruba.

- Jazz Enthusiast: Beyond basketball, Abdul-Jabbar is a passionate jazz drummer and has even released several albums.

- Social Activist: Abdul-Jabbar is a prominent voice for social justice and has spoken out against racism and discrimination throughout his career.

- Scholar and Author: Abdul-Jabbar holds a Master's degree in history and has authored several books, including his autobiography, "Giant Steps."

- The Unstoppable Skyhook: Abdul-Jabbar's signature shot, the skyhook, was nearly impossible to block due to its high release point and smooth release. He perfected this shot over years of practice, making it an unstoppable weapon in his arsenal.

- Longevity and Durability: Abdul-Jabbar played 20 seasons in the NBA, the most of any player at the time. He remained remarkably healthy throughout his career, missing only 50 games total.

- Quiet Leadership: Abdul-Jabbar was not known for his flamboyant personality, but he was a respected leader on the court and in the locker room. His quiet strength and unwavering dedication were instrumental in the Lakers' championship success.

- Post-Basketball Success: Abdul-Jabbar has enjoyed a successful career beyond basketball as a coach, author, and film producer.

- Mentor and Inspiration: Abdul-Jabbar has been a mentor and inspiration to countless young athletes, including Kobe Bryant, who he coached during his early years in the NBA.

A Giant of the Game

Kareem Abdul-Jabbar's legacy extends far beyond his statistical achievements. His commitment to excellence, his passion for social justice, and his dedication to learning make him a true role model for athletes and individuals alike. His impact on the game of basketball will be felt for generations to come.

A Kareem Abdul-Jabbar Story

Kareem Abdul-Jabbar, despite his towering stature and intimidating presence, had a dry sense of humor and a penchant for the absurd. Here's a funny story that exemplifies his playful side.

During a road trip, the Los Angeles Lakers were staying in a hotel known for its notoriously thin walls. Kareem, being a man of routine, liked to unwind in his room by listening to opera music at night. However, the volume of his music became a source of irritation for his teammates, especially the more light-sleeping ones.

One night, after enduring another evening of booming opera, Magic Johnson decided to take action. He slipped into Kareem's room and, with a mischievous grin, replaced his opera CDs with a collection of polka music.

The next morning, Kareem emerged from his room looking bewildered and slightly disheveled. He approached Magic and, with a deadpan expression, uttered the words, "Magic, I've never heard Wagner sound so much like polka music in my life."

The entire team erupted in laughter, including Kareem himself. He understood the playful prank and even admitted that the polka music, though unexpected, was strangely entertaining.

This incident reveals Kareem's ability to find humor in unexpected situations and to laugh at himself. It also showcases the camaraderie and playful spirit within the Lakers team, highlighting the importance of off-court bonds and shared experiences in building a championship-winning culture.

Chapter 4: Bill Russell

"The Ultimate Winner and a Defensive Powerhouse"

Bill Russell, the centerpiece of the Boston Celtics dynasty, stands as a titan of basketball history. His unmatched dominance in rebounding and defense, combined with his unwavering leadership, paved the way for an unparalleled 11 NBA championships in 13 seasons. But beyond the accolades and championships, intriguing details and rare facts further reveal the depth of his basketball genius and his enduring impact on the game.

Statistical Prowess

- 11 NBA Championships (1957, 1959-1966, 1968, 1969 - all with the Boston Celtics)
- 5 NBA Most Valuable Player Awards (1958, 1961-1963, 1965)
- 12 NBA All-Star appearances:
- 11 All-NBA First Team selections
- 4 NBA Rebounding Titles
- 5-time NBA Defensive Player of the Year (the award didn't officially begin until 1969)
- 2 Olympic Gold Medals (1956, 1964)

Interesting Facts

- Overcoming Adversity: From facing racial discrimination throughout his career to battling injuries, Russell never allowed adversity to deter him. He used these challenges to fuel his passion and determination.

- Dominant Rebounder: Russell's rebounding prowess was legendary. He holds the NBA record for most rebounds in a game (51) and the second-highest career total (21,620 rebounds).

- Defensive Genius: Russell revolutionized the game with his defensive strategies, focusing on team defense and positioning rather than individual stats. He led the Celtics to the league's best defensive record for eight consecutive seasons.

- Unselfish Leader: Russell was a true team player who prioritized winning over individual accolades. He famously once said, "The most important measure of a player is his contribution to winning."

- Social Activist: Russell was a vocal advocate for civil rights and racial equality. He participated in marches and boycotts, even refusing to play in the 1961 exhibition game in Lexington, Kentucky, due to the city's segregation laws.

- Coaching Success: In 1966, Russell became the first African American coach in a major American professional sport. He led the Celtics to two NBA championships in his coaching tenure.

- Business Ventures: Russell was a successful entrepreneur after his basketball career. He founded a company that manufactured athletic wear and footwear.

- Philanthropy: Russell is a dedicated philanthropist who supports various charities, including the NAACP and the Bill Russell Legacy Foundation.

- Reluctant Icon: Russell was known for his humble nature and preferred to stay out of the spotlight. He often criticized the media and the focus on individual players rather than the team.

A Legacy of Excellence

Bill Russell's impact on the game of basketball extends far beyond his on-court accomplishments. He is a symbol of resilience, leadership, and dedication. His legacy continues to inspire players and fans alike, reminding us that true greatness lies in teamwork, sacrifice, and unwavering commitment to achieving the ultimate goal: winning.

A Bill Russell Story

Bill Russell, despite his serious demeanor and immense success as a basketball player, possessed a dry wit and a knack for surprising people with his humor. Here's a funny story that demonstrates his playful side.

During a press conference after winning one of his numerous NBA championships, Russell was bombarded with questions from reporters about his impressive achievements. One particularly inquisitive reporter asked, "Bill, what do you think is the biggest difference between you and Wilt Chamberlain?"

Russell, known for his brief and often humorous responses, paused for a moment and then replied with a straight face, "Well, for starters, I have 11 championships, and he has none."

The room erupted in laughter, catching the curious reporter off guard. Russell's dry wit and ability to deflect attention with humor were trademarks of his personality. This story highlights his comfortable presence under pressure and his ability to make light even in high-stakes situations.

Here's another funny story about Bill Russell that you might enjoy.

One day, during a practice session, Russell noticed a young rookie struggling with a particular drill. The rookie, frustrated and discouraged, was ready to give up. Russell, always the mentor, approached him and offered some advice.

With a mischievous twinkle in his eye, Russell said, "Son, don't worry. I've been playing this game for a long time, and I still can't do that drill either."

The rookie, initially surprised, couldn't help but laugh. Russell's playful encouragement and willingness to admit his own limitations helped ease the rookie's pressure and boost his confidence. This story exemplifies Russell's leadership style, which was built on humor, humility, and a genuine desire to see his teammates succeed.

Chapter 5: Wilt Chamberlain

"A Force of Nature and Basketball Legend"

Wilt Chamberlain, the "Big Dipper," was a dominant force in the NBA who redefined the game with his unmatched athleticism, scoring prowess, and rebounding dominance. His name is etched in basketball history with a plethora of records, including the most points scored in a single game (100) and the most rebounds in a career (23,924). However, delving deeper reveals fascinating details and rare facts that further illuminate the extraordinary talent and impact of this legendary player.

Statistical Highlights

- 100 points in a single game (March 2, 1962): This feat remains the NBA's single-game scoring record and is considered one of the most iconic moments in basketball history.

- 55 rebounds in a single game (Nov. 24, 1960): This record for the most rebounds in a game also stands as a testament to Chamberlain's unparalleled dominance on the boards.

- 23,924 career rebounds: Chamberlain still holds the record for the most total rebounds in NBA history, showcasing his incredible ability to control the paint.

- 7-time scoring champion: Chamberlain led the league in scoring seven times, averaging over 30 points per game on three occasions.

- 4-time rebounding champion: Chamberlain's rebounding dominance was unmatched, leading the league in rebounding four times throughout his career.
- 2-time NBA champion (1967 with Philadelphia 76ers, 1972 with Los Angeles Lakers): While not known for his team championships, Chamberlain proved his ability to win at the highest level.

Interesting Facts

- Never fouled out of a game: Despite playing in an era known for its physicality, Chamberlain's incredible footwork and basketball IQ allowed him to avoid fouling out of any of his 1,045 career games.
- Track and field star: Chamberlain was a talented athlete beyond basketball, holding the world record in the shot put for several years and competing in the 1956 Olympic Games.
- Volleyball prowess: Chamberlain was also a skilled volleyball player, playing professionally in the International Volleyball Association for two seasons.
- Business ventures: Chamberlain was a successful businessman after his basketball career, investing in various ventures, including a Harlem Globetrotters franchise and a chain of restaurants.
- Musical aspirations: Chamberlain pursued a singing career after retiring from basketball, releasing several albums in the 1970s.
- Movie appearances: Chamberlain appeared in several Hollywood films, including "Conan the Destroyer" and "The Fish that Saved Pittsburgh."

- Humanitarian efforts: Chamberlain was a dedicated philanthropist, supporting numerous charities and causes throughout his life.

- Unique personality: Chamberlain was known for his flamboyant personality and outspoken nature, often making headlines for his off-court antics.

- Unmatched athleticism: Chamberlain's combination of size, strength, and athleticism was unmatched in his era, making him a truly dominant force on the court.

A Legacy of Innovation

Wilt Chamberlain's impact on the game of basketball goes far beyond his statistics and records. He redefined the role of the center and pushed the boundaries of what was thought possible on the court. His legacy continues to inspire players and fans alike, reminding us that raw talent combined with unwavering dedication can create a force of nature that can change the game forever.

Wilt Chamberlain Stories

Wilt Chamberlain, known for his larger-than-life personality and dominant presence on the court, also possessed a playful side and a knack for self-deprecating humor. Here are two funny stories that exemplify his sense of humor.

Story 1

During a game, Chamberlain was being guarded by a significantly smaller player. After backing down his defender with ease and scoring a basket,

Chamberlain turned to the crowd and said, "You know, it's really not fair. I'm 7'1", and he's 5'10". It's like taking candy from a baby."

The crowd burst into laughter, appreciating Chamberlain's playful jab at his own physical advantage. This story highlights his confidence and humor in acknowledging his unique physical attributes.

Story 2

One day, a reporter asked Chamberlain, "Wilt, do you think you're the best player in the world?"

Chamberlain, without missing a beat, replied, "I don't know. I haven't played myself yet."

This witty response showcases Chamberlain's sense of humor and his ability to deflect attention with self-deprecating jokes. While he knew his own talent, he also remained humble and avoided boasting about his achievements.

These stories illustrate that despite being one of the most dominant athletes in basketball history, Wilt Chamberlain possessed a playful and humorous personality. He knew how to use humor to connect with people and to keep himself grounded, even in the face of immense success.

Chapter 6: LeBron James

"The King of All-Around Excellence"

LeBron James, nicknamed "King James," has cemented his place among the greatest basketball players of all time. His exceptional athleticism, combined with his remarkable passing vision and basketball IQ, has made him a dominant force on the court for over two decades. Let's delve deeper into his career and explore some rare facts that shed light on the legend he has become.

Statistical Prowess

- 4 NBA Championships (2012 with Miami Heat, 2013, 2016 with Cleveland Cavaliers, 2020 with Los Angeles Lakers)
- 4 NBA Most Valuable Player Awards (2009, 2010, 2012, 2013)
- 4 NBA Finals MVP Awards (2012, 2013, 2016, 2020)
- 19 NBA All-Star appearances
- 13 All-NBA First Team selections
- 6 NBA All-Defensive First Team selections
- NBA's All-Time Leading Scorer in the playoffs (7,631 points)
- 4 Olympic Gold Medals (2008, 2012, 2016, 2020)

Interesting Facts

- Precocious Talent: LeBron's exceptional talent was evident from a young age. He was featured on the cover of Sports Illustrated at the age of 17, dubbed "The Chosen One."

- Versatility: LeBron is one of the most versatile players in NBA history, possessing the ability to score, rebound, and pass at an elite level. He is often referred to as a "triple-double machine" for his consistent ability to achieve double-digit figures in three statistical categories.

- High School Phenom: During his high school career, LeBron led St. Vincent-St. Mary High School to three state championships, becoming the first junior to be named Gatorade National Player of the Year.

- Business Acumen: LeBron has been a successful businessman beyond the basketball court, launching his own clothing line, production company, and various other ventures.

- Philanthropy: LeBron is a dedicated philanthropist who supports various charitable causes, focusing on education and empowering youth through his foundation.

- Longevity: Despite being in his 20th season, LeBron remains a dominant force in the NBA, showcasing remarkable durability and a commitment to staying at the peak of his physical condition.

- Global Icon: LeBron has transcended the sport of basketball and is a global icon. He has leveraged his platform to speak out on social issues and inspire millions around the world.

- Family Man: LeBron is a devoted family man, often crediting his wife and children for his motivation and success.

- Breaking Records: LeBron continues to break records throughout his career. He recently surpassed Kareem Abdul-Jabbar as the NBA's all-time leading scorer, solidifying his place as one of the greatest scorers in league history.

A Legacy of Inspiration

LeBron James continues to inspire basketball fans across the globe. His unwavering dedication to the game, combined with his commitment to his family and his passion for giving back to the community, makes him a role model for athletes and individuals alike. His legacy as one of the greatest basketball players of all time is secure, and his impact on the sport continues to grow with each passing season.

Lebron James Stories

LeBron James, known for his serious on-court demeanor and leadership, also possesses a playful side and a knack for witty comebacks. Here are two funny stories that demonstrate his comedic timing.

Story 1

During a game, LeBron was arguing with a referee about a foul call. The referee, trying to assert his authority, said, "LeBron, I'm just trying to do my job."

Without missing a beat, LeBron replied, "Well, I'm just trying to win a championship."

The entire arena erupted in laughter, even the referee couldn't help but crack a smile. This story highlights LeBron's confidence and his ability to use humor to deflect tension and defuse heated situations.

Story 2

During a media interview, a reporter asked LeBron, "LeBron, what is it like to be considered one of the greatest basketball players of all time?" LeBron, with a playful smile, replied, "I don't know, ask my barber. He's the one who cuts all the greatest."

This witty response showcases LeBron's ability to use humor to deflect self-praise and remain humble despite his immense achievements. He understands the importance of staying grounded and not taking himself too seriously, even when facing high expectations and constant scrutiny.

These stories demonstrate that despite being one of the most decorated athletes in basketball history, LeBron James possesses a playful and humorous personality. He uses humor to connect with people, keep himself grounded, and navigate the pressures of being in the spotlight.

Chapter 7: Magic Johnson

"The Point God and Showman"

Earvin "Magic" Johnson, the "Point God" and a key architect of the iconic "Showtime Lakers," revolutionized the point guard position with his unparalleled passing vision, electrifying no-look passes, and infectious charisma. Beyond the dazzling assists and championship rings, interesting facts and lesser-known aspects reveal the depth of his talent and his enduring influence on the game.

Statistical Highlights

- 5 NBA Championships (1980, 1982, 1985, 1987, 1988 - all with Los Angeles Lakers)
- 3 NBA Most Valuable Player Awards (1987, 1989, 1990)
- 3 NBA Finals MVP Awards (1980, 1982, 1987)
- 12 NBA All-Star appearances
- 9 All-NBA First Team selections
- 5 NBA All-Defensive First Team selections
- NBA's All-Time Assists Leader (10,141 assists)
- 2 Olympic Gold Medals (1979, 1992)

Interesting Facts

- Multi-Positional Master: In his rookie season, Magic famously played all five positions in the championship-clinching game, showcasing his versatility and basketball IQ.

- College Basketball Legend: Magic led Michigan State University to the NCAA championship in 1979, solidifying his status as a collegiate legend.

- Showtime Spectacle: Magic's flamboyant passing and leadership were instrumental in creating the "Showtime" Lakers, a team renowned for its fast-paced, high-scoring offense.

- HIV Diagnosis and Advocacy: In 1991, Magic announced his HIV diagnosis, becoming a prominent advocate for HIV/AIDS awareness and education.

- Business Success: Magic has been a successful entrepreneur, founding Magic Johnson Enterprises, which invests in various businesses and has a net worth exceeding $1 billion.

- Broadcasting Career: Magic served as a commentator for NBA games and hosted his own talk show, demonstrating his charisma and communication skills beyond the court.

- Passionate Mentor: Magic has mentored numerous young players, including Kobe Bryant, sharing his wisdom and experience to help them reach their full potential.

- Community Involvement: Magic is actively involved in various philanthropic initiatives, focusing on empowering communities and promoting education.

- Cultural Icon: Magic transcended basketball, becoming a global icon and influencing popular culture through his fashion sense, music videos, and public appearances.

A Legacy of Innovation

Magic Johnson revolutionized the game of basketball with his groundbreaking style of play. He redefined the role of the point guard, showcasing the importance of passing and vision as key ingredients for success. His enduring legacy extends beyond his statistics, as he remains a true icon who inspires generations of players and fans with his talent, charisma, and commitment to making a positive impact on the world.

Magic Johnson Stories

Magic Johnson, known for his infectious smile and charismatic personality, was also a master of practical jokes and playful pranks. Here are two funny stories that showcase his sense of humor.

Story 1

During a road trip, Magic noticed that his teammate, Kareem Abdul-Jabbar, was always reading serious books on philosophy and history. Magic, being the playful prankster, decided to replace Kareem's book with a comic book.

The next morning, Kareem opened his book with a confused expression. He turned to Magic and said, "Magic, I don't remember ordering this children's book."

Magic, barely able to contain his laughter, replied, "Kareem, sometimes you need to lighten up and read something fun."

This prank exemplifies Magic's ability to connect with his teammates through humor and to bring laughter even in the midst of a demanding season. It also highlights Kareem's good sportsmanship and willingness to laugh at himself, even when tricked by his mischievous teammate.

Story 2

One day, Magic was walking through the airport with his teammates when he spotted a group of young children eagerly waiting for autographs. Magic, being the showman, decided to put on a little show for the kids. He walked up to them with a serious expression and said, "Excuse me, young fans, do you know who I am?"

The children, confused, shook their heads.

Magic then pulled out a large, fake afro wig from his bag and put it on his head. With a grin, he said, "Well, I'm Kareem Abdul-Jabbar!"

The children burst out laughing, realizing they had been tricked by the playful magician. This story exemplifies Magic's ability to connect with children and to bring joy through his humor and playful antics. It also highlights his charisma and his knack for creating memorable moments for his fans.

These stories demonstrate that Magic Johnson's playful personality was an integral part of his success and popularity. He used humor to connect with people, build relationships, and create a positive and enjoyable atmosphere within the team. His playful spirit and infectious laughter made him a beloved figure on and off the court.

Chapter 8: Larry Bird

"The Hick from French Lick"

More than just a basketball player, "The Hick from French Lick" transcended the sport with his exceptional skill, unwavering determination, and iconic persona. Let's delve into his remarkable career, exploring his impressive statistics and intriguing facts that solidify his legacy as one of the greatest players ever.

Statistical Dominance

- 3 NBA Championships (1981, 1984, 1986 - all with the Boston Celtics)
- 3 NBA Most Valuable Player Awards (1984, 1985, 1986)
- 2 NBA Finals MVP Awards (1984, 1986)
- 12 NBA All-Star appearances
- 10 All-NBA First Team selections
- 5 All-NBA Second Team selections
- 3 All-Defensive First Team selections
- 9 times led the NBA in three-point percentage
- Career averages of 24.3 points per game, 6.3 assists per game, and 10.0 rebounds per game

Interesting Facts and Trivia

- Unconventional Shooting Form: Despite his unorthodox shooting technique, Larry Bird was a master of the craft, boasting a career three-point percentage of 39.8%, placing him among the best in NBA history.

- Lefty Legend: Though naturally right-handed, Bird learned to shoot left-handed as a child to avoid injuring his dominant hand. This unique skill became his signature shot and a vital part of his offensive arsenal.

- Triple-Double Machine: While primarily known for his scoring, Bird was a versatile player who contributed significantly in rebounds and assists. He recorded an impressive 59 triple-doubles throughout his career, showcasing his all-around talent.

- Trash-Talking Master: Bird's on-court persona was defined by his witty and often humorous trash-talk. He used his words to unsettle opponents and gain a mental edge, adding to his competitive spirit and leadership.

- From Small Town to Superstardom: Born and raised in French Lick, Indiana, a town with a population of less than 2,000, Bird's journey resonated with players and fans, inspiring individuals from small backgrounds to achieve greatness.

- Business Savvy: Beyond basketball, Bird displayed entrepreneurial acumen. He successfully served as the president of basketball operations for the Indiana Pacers, leading them to the NBA Finals in 2000.

- Cultural Icon: Bird transcended the sport, becoming a household name and cultural icon. His unique style, competitive drive, and humble personality made him an inspiration and role model for generations of athletes and fans.

A Legacy of Brilliance

Larry Bird's career is marked by exceptional achievements, unwavering dedication, and a unique personality. He dominated the game with his skill and vision, captivating audiences with his trademark shooting touch and competitive spirit. His impact on basketball goes far beyond statistics and championships, solidifying his place as one of the greatest players to ever grace the court. His legacy continues to inspire athletes and fans alike, reminding us that talent, hard work, and a genuine love for the game can lead to extraordinary achievements.

Beyond the Stats

a. Unparalleled Shooting: Bird was a marksman from anywhere on the court, possessing an unorthodox but deadly shooting form. He is widely considered one of the greatest shooters in NBA history, holding a career average of 44.1% from the field and 39.8% from beyond the arc.

b. Exceptional Passing Vision: Bird wasn't just a scorer. He was a master of the no-look pass and possessed an uncanny ability to anticipate plays and find his teammates for open shots. His vision and passing skills made him the ultimate floor general, guiding the Celtics offense to numerous victories.

c. Clutch Performer: Bird thrived under pressure. He was known for his icy demeanor and his ability to hit clutch shots in high-stakes situations. His confidence and calmness under pressure were instrumental in the Celtics' championship runs.

d. Versatile Defender: Though not the most athletic player, Bird was a surprisingly effective defender. He used his intelligence and anticipation skills to read plays and disrupt opposing offenses.

e. Relentless Competitor: Bird's competitive spirit was legendary. He hated to lose and pushed himself and his teammates to be their best. This intensity fueled his success and drove him to achieve greatness.

Larry Bird Stories

Larry Bird, known for his "Hick from French Lick" persona and his laid-back demeanor, also possessed a dry wit and a penchant for playful trash talk. Here are two funny stories that illustrate his sense of humor.

Story 1

During a game, Bird was matched up against Michael Jordan, arguably the greatest trash talker in NBA history. Jordan, always trying to get into his opponent's head, said to Bird, "I'm going to cross you up so bad you'll need a map to find your way back to the bench."

Bird, without missing a beat, replied, "That's okay, Michael. I'll just follow the smell of your cologne."

This witty response showcases Bird's ability to deflect trash talk with humor and to remain unfazed by even the most intimidating opponents. It also highlights his confidence and his dry sense of humor, which often left others surprised and amused.

Story 2

During a practice session, Bird was struggling with his shot. His teammates were surprised, as Bird was known for his incredible shooting accuracy. One of his teammates, trying to offer encouragement, said, "Hey, Larry, what's wrong? You usually make those shots in your sleep." Bird paused for a moment and then said, "Well, I must be sleepwalking tonight then."

This self-deprecating humor exemplifies Bird's ability to laugh at himself, even when faced with challenges or setbacks. It highlights his humble nature and his ability to stay grounded despite his immense talent.

These stories demonstrate that Larry Bird was much more than just a skilled basketball player. He possessed a unique personality that combined a dry wit, a laid-back demeanor, and a competitive spirit. His humor and playful nature made him a popular figure among fans and teammates alike, adding another dimension to his legacy as one of the greatest basketball players of all time.

Chapter 9: Tim Duncan

"A Statistical and Historical Powerhouse"

Tim Duncan, affectionately nicknamed "The Big Fundamental," was the bedrock of the San Antonio Spurs dynasty, a model of consistency and excellence on both ends of the court. His statistical dominance, coupled with his unwavering dedication and quiet leadership, cemented his place among the greatest power forwards ever to grace the NBA.

Statistical Prowess

- 5 NBA Championships (1999, 2003, 2005, 2007, 2014 - all with the San Antonio Spurs)
- 2 NBA Most Valuable Player Awards (2002, 2003)
- 3 NBA Finals MVP Awards (1999, 2003, 2005)
- 15 NBA All-Star appearances
- 10 All-NBA First Team selections
- 5 All-NBA Second Team selections
- 8 NBA All-Defensive First Team selections
- 15 times led the NBA in Defensive Win Shares
- Career averages of 19.0 points per game, 11.1 rebounds per game, and 3.0 assists per game

Interesting Facts and Trivia

- Dominating Defense: Duncan's defensive prowess was legendary. He possessed exceptional footwork, positioning, and timing, earning him the nickname "The Big Fundamental." He revolutionized the power forward position with his ability to guard multiple positions and anchor the Spurs' defensive scheme.

- Unassuming Leader: Unlike many other superstars, Duncan shied away from the spotlight and preferred to lead by example. His quiet demeanor, work ethic, and unwavering dedication served as an inspiration for his teammates and a cornerstone of the Spurs' success.

- Model of Consistency: Throughout his 19-year career, Duncan rarely missed games and maintained a remarkably consistent level of play. He was known for his meticulous preparation, attention to detail, and unwavering commitment to his craft.

- Longevity and Durability: Playing in an era known for its physicality, Duncan managed to avoid major injuries and play at an elite level well into his 30s. His remarkable durability and consistent performance are a testament to his dedication to fitness and conditioning.

- Gifted Athlete: Despite his "Big Fundamental" nickname, Duncan was also a skilled passer and possessed a soft touch around the rim. He developed his offensive skillset throughout his career, making him a difficult matchup for any defender.

- International Success: Duncan was a key member of the United States National Team, winning gold medals in the 1998 FIBA World Championship and the 2000 Olympic Games. He is considered one of the greatest international players of all time.

- Philanthropic Endeavors: Beyond basketball, Duncan is a dedicated philanthropist. He has supported various charitable causes, including the Tim Duncan Foundation, which focuses on providing educational opportunities for underprivileged youth.

A Legacy of Excellence

Tim Duncan's career is a testament to hard work, dedication, and unwavering passion for the game. His statistical achievements and championship rings speak volumes about his talent and dominance. However, his most significant legacy lies in his leadership, sportsmanship, and commitment to excellence. He redefined the power forward position and inspired generations of players with his quiet intensity and unwavering dedication to the craft. The "Big Fundamental" will forever be remembered as one of the greatest basketball players to ever walk onto the court.

Tim Duncan Stories

Tim Duncan, known for his quiet demeanor and "Big Fundamental" approach to the game, also had a dry wit and a playful side that occasionally peeked through. Here are two funny stories that showcase his sense of humor.

Story 1

During a practice session, Tim Duncan was working on his free throws. He was known for his unorthodox shooting form, which involved a one-handed release and a bit of a hitch. One of his teammates, trying to be helpful, said, "Tim, maybe you should try changing your free throw form. It looks a bit awkward."

Duncan, without missing a beat, replied, "It's not awkward, it's just effective."

This story exemplifies Duncan's confidence in his own abilities and his refusal to conform to conventional standards. He understood that his unconventional style, despite its unorthodox appearance, worked for him and helped him excel on the court.

Story 2

One day, a reporter asked Tim Duncan, "Tim, how do you manage to stay so calm and focused under pressure, even during the most intense moments of the game?"

Duncan, with a deadpan expression, replied, "Well, I just remind myself that it's just a game. It's not brain surgery."

This witty response highlights Duncan's ability to deflect attention and to maintain a sense of perspective. He understood the importance of not taking things too seriously and of keeping a calm and focused mindset, even in the heat of competition.

While Tim Duncan's humor was often subtle and dry, it was no less effective in bringing laughter and lightheartedness to the team environment. His playful jabs and witty remarks, delivered with his characteristic deadpan expression, endeared him to his teammates and fans alike, revealing another layer to his personality beyond the stoic and focused demeanor he displayed on the court.

Chapter 10: Kobe Bryant

"The Black Mamba"

Kobe Bryant, "The Black Mamba," was a force of nature on the court, captivating audiences with his electrifying athleticism, relentless scoring, and unyielding spirit. His remarkable career, filled with championships, accolades, and unforgettable moments, cemented his legacy as one of the greatest shooting guards and competitors in NBA history.

Statistical Brilliance

- 5 NBA Championships (2000-2002, 2009, 2010 - all with the Los Angeles Lakers)
- 2 NBA Finals MVP Awards (2009, 2010)
- 1 NBA Most Valuable Player Award (2008)
- 18 NBA All-Star appearances
- 15 All-NBA First Team selections
- 11 All-Defensive First Team selections
- 3 times led the NBA in scoring
- Career averages of 25.0 points per game, 5.2 rebounds per game, and 4.7 assists per game

Interesting Facts and Trivia

- Unstoppable Scorer: Kobe possessed an unmatched offensive arsenal, capable of scoring from anywhere on the court with his dazzling footwork, deadly fadeaway, and acrobatic finishes. He is the NBA's third all-time leading scorer with 33,643 points, a testament to his scoring prowess and longevity.

- Mamba Mentality: Kobe's relentless drive and competitive spirit were legendary. He embraced the "Mamba Mentality," a philosophy of constant improvement, unwavering focus, and a ruthless pursuit of excellence. This mentality instilled an infectious energy and a winning attitude within himself and his teammates.

- Olympic Gold Medalist: Kobe represented the United States on the international stage, winning gold medals in the 2008 and 2012 Olympic Games. He showcased his versatility and leadership skills on the international stage, further solidifying his status as one of the best players in the world.

- Cultural Icon: Kobe's impact transcended basketball. He became a global icon whose influence extended far beyond the sport. His fashion sense, business ventures, and philanthropic endeavors cemented his place as a cultural phenomenon.

- Mentorship and Inspiration: Kobe served as a mentor and inspiration to countless aspiring athletes. He shared his wisdom and experience through camps, speeches, and various initiatives, motivating young players to pursue their dreams with passion and dedication.

- Post-Retirement Success: After his retirement from basketball, Kobe explored his creative side, winning an Academy Award for the animated short film "Dear Basketball." He also invested in various ventures, including a multimedia production company and a sports drink company.

- Tragic Loss: Kobe's tragic passing in 2020 left a void in the basketball world and beyond. He is remembered as a talented athlete, passionate competitor, and loving father, whose legacy continues to inspire generations to come.

A Legacy of Dominance and Inspiration

Kobe Bryant's career was a tapestry of remarkable achievements and unwavering dedication. His statistics will forever be etched in history, but his true legacy lies in his infectious spirit, relentless pursuit of excellence, and the inspiration he provided to athletes and individuals worldwide. The "Black Mamba" will forever be remembered as a basketball legend, a cultural icon, and a constant reminder that hard work, passion, and relentless drive can lead to greatness both on and off the court.

Kobe Byrant Stories

Kobe Bryant had a reputation for being intensely focused and driven on the court. However, there are also stories that reveal his playful side and sense of humor. Here are two examples.

Story 1

During a practice session, Kobe was working on his post moves against his teammate, Pau Gasol. Gasol, a skilled defender himself, was giving Kobe a tough time. After one particularly successful defensive play, Gasol looked at Kobe and said, "Kobe, you're not getting past me today." Kobe, with a grin, replied, "Pau, just remember, there's a reason why they call me the 'Black Mamba.' Snakes are known for their patience and their ability to strike at the perfect moment."

Gasol laughed, knowing that Kobe was just trying to get under his skin and maintain his competitive spirit. This story highlights Kobe's playful competitiveness and his ability to use humor to motivate himself and his teammates.

Story 2

One day, a reporter asked Kobe about the pressure of being compared to Michael Jordan, arguably the greatest basketball player of all time. Kobe, known for his confidence and ambition, replied with a smile:

"I don't feel pressure to be like Michael Jordan. I'm not trying to be the next Michael Jordan. I'm trying to be the first Kobe Bryant."

This response showcases Kobe's self-assuredness and his belief in his own unique talent. He understood that while Jordan was a legend, he wouldn't reach his full potential by trying to imitate him. He wanted to create his own legacy and be remembered as one of the greats in his own right.

These stories demonstrate that Kobe Bryant was more than just a serious athlete. He also possessed a playful side and a dry wit that often surfaced off the court. His humor and competitiveness added a new dimension to his personality and endeared him to his fans. He wasn't just a basketball player; he was a complex and multifaceted individual who left a lasting impact on the game and on everyone who knew him.

Chapter 11: Shaquille O'Neal

"The Shaq Attack"

Shaquille O'Neal, affectionately known as "Shaq," reigned supreme in the NBA paint during his prime, leaving opponents trembling in his wake. With a combination of sheer size, unparalleled strength, and surprising agility, Shaq was an unstoppable force, rewriting the narrative of center play and carving his name into basketball history.

Statistical Prowess

- 4 NBA Championships (3 with the Los Angeles Lakers: 2000-2002; 1 with the Miami Heat: 2006)
- 3 Finals MVP Awards (2000, 2001, 2006)
- 1 NBA MVP Award (2000)
- 15 NBA All-Star appearances
- 14 All-NBA First Team selections
- 3 NBA All-Defensive First Team selections
- 2 times led the NBA in scoring
- Career averages of 23.7 points per game, 10.9 rebounds per game, and 2.3 assists per game

Beyond the Stats

- Unmatched Physical Dominance: Shaq's combination of size (7'1", 325 pounds) and strength was unmatched. He routinely overpowered defenders, dominating the paint with his booming dunks and unstoppable post moves.

- Surprisingly Agile: Despite his imposing stature, Shaq possessed unexpected agility and footwork, allowing him to navigate the paint and finish around the rim with incredible efficiency.

- Relentless Competitor: Shaq brought an unmatched intensity and competitive spirit to the court. His relentless drive and passion for the game were infectious, inspiring teammates and intimidating opponents.

- Showman and Entertainer: Shaq's larger-than-life personality extended beyond the court. He embraced his role as a showman, engaging with fans and media with his humor, charisma, and infectious laughter.

- Business Acumen: Beyond basketball, Shaq demonstrated remarkable business acumen. He invested in various ventures, including restaurants, music labels, and video games, solidifying his success outside the sports world.

- Philanthropy and Community Involvement: Shaq is a dedicated philanthropist, supporting various causes and initiatives focused on empowering youth and promoting education.

- Global Icon: Shaq's influence transcended the basketball world. He became a global icon, recognized for his athletic achievements, personality, and business success.

A Legacy of Domination and Entertainment

Shaquille O'Neal's career was a force of nature. His statistical dominance, unmatched physical presence, and infectious personality redefined the center position and captivated audiences worldwide. He leaves behind a legacy of dominance, entertainment, and philanthropy, inspiring generations of athletes and fans to dream big, achieve greatness, and embrace life with a smile. The "Shaq Attack" will forever be remembered as one of the most iconic and unforgettable figures in basketball history.

Shaquille O'Neal Stories

Shaq, despite his intimidating size and serious demeanor on the court, was also known for his playful personality and infectious laughter. Here are two stories that showcase his sense of humor.

Story 1

During a post-game interview, Shaq was asked about a particularly dominant performance where he scored over 40 points. The reporter, trying to get a reaction, said, "Shaq, some people are saying you're unstoppable. What do you think?"

Shaq, with a mischievous grin, replied, "Well, I haven't stopped yet, have I?"

This confident response and playful jab at the question exemplify Shaq's self-awareness and his ability to deflect attention with humor. He knew his own talent and didn't shy away from acknowledging it, but he also did so in a way that was lighthearted and playful.

Story 2

One day, Shaq was walking through the airport with his teammates when he spotted a group of young children staring at him with wide eyes and open mouths. Shaq, being the entertainer, decided to put on a little show for them.

He walked up to the children and, in his booming voice, said, "Hello everyone! Do you know who I am?"

The children, hesitantly, shook their heads.

Shaq then put his hand on his chest and said, "I'm Superman!"

The children, confused but amused, looked at each other and then back at Shaq. He then winked at them and continued walking, leaving the children with a smile on their faces and a memorable encounter with the "Shaq-Man."

This story highlights Shaq's playful nature and his ability to connect with people of all ages. He understood the power of laughter and used humor to bring joy and entertain those around him, even strangers. His playful spirit and larger-than-life personality made him a beloved figure both on and off the court.

These stories demonstrate that Shaq was more than just a dominant basketball player. He was also a fun-loving and charismatic individual who used humor to connect with people and leave a lasting impression.

His playful antics and infectious laughter made him a beloved figure among fans and teammates alike, adding another dimension to his legacy as one of the greatest centers in NBA history.

9 781774 818664